EASTER JOKES FOR KIDS!

HUNDREDS OF HILARIOUS EASTER JOKES INSIDE!

Jacky Jay

With hundreds of really funny, hilarious jokes, Easter Jokes For Kids promises hours of fun for the whole family!

Includes brand new, original Easter Knock Knock Jokes that will have the kids (and adults!) in fits of laughter in no time!

Suitable for all ages from 5-12. Perfect for the young comedians in your family!

These jokes are so funny it's going to be hard not to laugh! Just wait until you hear the giggles and laughter!

Have a very Happy Easter!

Books by Jacky Jay

To see all the latest books by
Jacky Jay just go to

jackyjay.com

Contents

Silly Easter Jokes!

What do you call a rabbit who tells jokes?
A funny bunny!

Which rabbit brings Easter Eggs to the fish in the sea?
The Oyster Bunny!

Knock knock.

Who's there?

Dish.

Dish who?

Dish is the best Easter Egg I have

ever seen!

Knock knock.

Who's there?

Kanye.

Kanye who?

Kanye give me a hand with this basket? It's really heavy!

Knock knock.

Who's there?

Chicken.

Chicken who?

I'm chicken under the trees and I can't find the eggs! Noooo!

What did the rabbit give his girlfriend?
A 14 carrot ring!

What did the Easter egg in a hurry say to the other egg?
Let's get cracking!

Knock knock.

Who's there?

Betty.

Betty who?

Betty you can't guess how many eggs

I have? 14! Yayyyy!

Knock knock.

Who's there?

Accordion.

Accordion who?

Accordion to the radio, the Easter Bunny will be here in 5 minutes!

Knock knock.

Who's there?

Troy.

Troy who?

Troy to find the candy before granddad eats it all!

Why did the egg hide?
It was a little chicken!

What do you call a chocolate Easter bunny
that was sunbaking?
A runny bunny!

Knock knock.

Who's there?

Needle.

Needle who?

Needle hand to eat your candy?

I'm still hungry!

Knock knock.

Who's there?

Zesty.

Zesty who?

Zesty right place for the Easter party?

Knock knock.

Who's there?

Lettuce.

Lettuce who?

Please lettuce in before our chocolate melts!

How did the Easter Bunny feel when he lost his Easter Basket?
Hopping mad!

What airline do rabbits use?
British Hare-ways!

Knock knock.

Who's there?

Aida.

Aida who?

Aida Easter egg for lunch and

now I'm full!

Knock knock.

Who's there?

Wilfred.

Wilfred who?

Wilfred be able to help me hunt eggs? I heard he's an expert!

Knock knock.

Who's there?

Alaska.

Alaska who?

Alaska you one more time! Please tell me where the Easter Bunny lives!

What do you get when you cross a rabbit with a leaf blower?

A hare dryer!

How does the Easter Bunny comb his fur?

With a hare brush!

Knock knock.

Who's there?

Van.

Van who?

Van are you going to let me in?

I'm hungry!!

Knock knock.

Who's there?

Juicy.

Juicy who?

Juicy the news! The Easter Bunny lives next door! Yayyyy!

Knock knock.

Who's there?

Udder.

Udder who?

You look a bit Udder the weather! Did you eat too much candy?

Who is the Easter Bunny's favorite movie actor?

Rabbit De Niro!

Why did the Easter Bunny leave school?

He was eggs-pelled!

Knock knock.

Who's there?

Harmony.

Harmony who?

Harmony Easter Eggs did you find?

I've got 27!

Knock knock.

Who's there?

Felix.

Felix who?

Felix my Easter egg one more time

he can buy me a new one!

Knock knock.

Who's there?

Handsome.

Handsome who?

Handsome chocolate over please

before I starve to death!

Why was the Easter Bunny scared of the comb?

He heard it was always teasing hares!

Why can't a T-Rex eat Easter eggs?

They are eggs-tinct!

Knock knock.

Who's there?

Weirdo.

Weirdo who?

Weirdo you think all the Easter eggs are hiding?

Knock knock.

Who's there?

Mushroom.

Mushroom who?

Do you have mushroom left in your basket? Mine is full!

Knock knock.

Who's there?

Ketchup.

Ketchup who?

Let's ketchup later on and have some chocolate!

What would you get if you crossed the Easter Bunny with a bumblebee?
A honey bunny!

What kind of cars do bunnies drive?
Hop rods!

Knock knock.

Who's there?

Wilma.

Wilma who?

Wilma Easter basket ever get full?

I've been hunting for 3 hours!

Knock knock.

Who's there?

Cupid.

Cupid who?

Cupid quiet!

I'm trying to sneak up on the Easter

Bunny! Shhhh.

Knock knock.

Who's there?

Sir.

Sir who?

Sir prise! I bet you weren't expecting

the Easter Bunny, were you?

What do you call a boy with
5 rabbits in his pockets?

Warren!

Why did the Easter Bunny say
Moooooooo?

He was learning another language!

Knock knock.

Who's there?

Alby.

Alby who?

Alby back in a minute, so just wait

there while I eat my candy!

Knock knock.

Who's there?

Sadie.

Sadie who?

Sadie magic word and the Easter Bunny will appear!

Knock knock.

Who's there?

Elsa.

Elsa who?

Who Elsa do you think it would be?

It's the Easter Bunny!

Funny Easter Jokes!

Why don't rabbits get hot
in the summertime?

They have hare conditioning!

Which side of the Easter Bunny
has the most fur?

The outside!

Knock knock.

Who's there?

Pudding.

Pudding who?

Pudding candy in your mouth!

Open wide!

Knock knock.

Who's there?

Seymour.

Seymour who?

I Seymour eggs when I

wear my glasses!

Knock knock.

Who's there?

Alpaca.

Alpaca who?

Alpaca my Easter basket so full I

will need a crane to lift it!

Knock knock.

Who's there?

Cannelloni.

Cannelloni who?

Cannelloni 5 bucks to buy some more candy? I ran out!

Knock knock.

Who's there?

CD.

CD who?

CD full Easter Basket? That's my lunch for tomorrow! Woo Hoo!

What did the 2 Easter bunnies do after they got married?

Lived hoppily ever after!

What did the naughty rabbit leave for Easter?

Devilled eggs!

Knock knock.

Who's there?

Avon.

Avon who?

Avon you to show me where

you hid the eggs!

Knock knock.

Who's there?

Toad.

Toad who?

I toad you the Easter Bunny

would come today! Yayyy!

Knock knock.

Who's there?

Arthur.

Arthur who?

Arthur any more eggs to decorate?

Come on! Just 1 more!

How did the Easter Bunny
find the lost train?
He followed it's tracks!

What do you call a rich rabbit?
A million-hare!

Knock knock.

Who's there?

Mint.

Mint who?

I mint to tell you - I ate

all of your chocolate!

Knock knock.

Who's there?

Athena.

Athena who?

Athena Bunny in your back yard!

Come and see!

Knock knock.

Who's there?

Quiet Tina.

Quiet Tina who?

Quiet Tina garden!

I'm trying to catch the Easter Bunny!

What is the Easter Bunny's favorite gym class?

Hare-obics!

How did the Easter Bunny get to New York?

On a hare-plane!

Knock knock.

Who's there?

Dozen.

Dozen who?

Dozen anybody want to give me some chocolate? I'm starving!

Knock knock.

Who's there?

Andrew.

Andrew who?

Andrew a very nice picture of the Easter Bunny! Do you want to see?

Knock knock.

Who's there?

Tweet.

Tweet who?

Would you like tweet some candy?

Yummy!

If a rabbit is born in Canada, grows up in Australia and dies in America, what is he?

Dead!

How did the Easter Bunny learn
to make a banana split?

He went to sundae school!

Knock knock.

Who's there?

Thor.

Thor who?

My arm is very Thor from carrying

this basket! Owwww!

Knock knock.

Who's there?

Wayne.

Wayne who?

It's going toWayne! Quick!

Find the eggs before they get wet!

Knock knock.

Who's there?

Emma.

Emma who?

Emma very hungry!

How about candy for lunch?

Which rabbits were famous bank robbers?
Bunny and Clyde!

Why was the Energizer Bunny sleeping?
He had a flat battery!

Knock knock.

Who's there?

Noah.

Noah who?

Noah good place to hide my giant

Easter Egg? How about in the toilet?

Knock knock.

Who's there?

Ben.

Ben who?

Ben away for years but now I'm back for Easter! Let's party!!

Knock knock.

Who's there?

Sister.

Sister who?

Sister right place for the Easter party tonight?

Why are Easter eggs never funny?
They tell bad yokes!

What do you call a rabbit in a kilt?
Hop scotch!

Knock knock.

Who's there?

Raymond.

Raymond who?

Raymond me to bring a

bigger basket next time!

So many eggs!

Knock knock.

Who's there?

Turnip.

Turnip who?

Turnip the music! Let's party!

Knock knock.

Who's there?

Zany.

Zany who?

Zany way we can fit more candy into my basket?

What do you call a rabbit who is angry over gettting burnt?

A hot cross bunny!

What do you call a happy rabbit?

A Hop-timist!

Knock knock.

Who's there?

Harvey.

Harvey who?

I hope you Harvey very good

Easter my good friend!

Knock knock.

Who's there?

Ken.

Ken who?

Ken you give me a hand with my

Easter Basket?

It weighs 100 pounds!

Knock knock.

Who's there?

Wooden Shoe.

Wooden shoe who?

Wooden shoe know it! The Easter

Bunny is here! Yayyyyy!

What's a bunnies' favorite TV show?

Hoppy Days!

Why did the Easter Bunny go to bed so early?

He was eggs-hausted!

Knock knock.

Who's there?

Zinc.

Zinc who?

I zinc chocolate is

tastier than broccoli!

Knock knock.

Who's there?

Fiddle.

Fiddle who?

Fiddle make you happy I'll keep telling Easter jokes!

Knock knock.

Who's there?

Harry.

Harry who?

Harry up! The eggs are melting!

Nooooooo!

Laugh Out Loud Easter Jokes!

What did the rabbit say to the carrot?
It's been nice gnawing you!

Where do rabbits work?
At IHOP restaurants!

Knock knock.

Who's there?

Claire.

Claire who?

Claire the way! Easter Bunny's here!

Knock knock.

Who's there?

Funnel.

Funnel who?

Funnel start in just a minute!

Easter egg hunt! Woohoo!

Knock knock.

Who's there?

Mustache.

Mustache who?

I mustache you a question.

Where did you put my Easter Eggs?

Why did the Easter Bunny leave college?
He failed the eggs-xams!

What do you call a chocolate
Easter Bunny that sunbakes?
A runny bunny!

Knock knock.

Who's there?

Ahmed.

Ahmed who?

Ahmed a mistake! Sorry!

Wrong house for the

Easter egg hunt!

Knock knock.

Who's there?

Jamaican.

Jamaican who?

Jamaican Easter dinner?

Yummy!

Knock knock.

Who's there?

Vitamin.

Vitamin who?

Vitamin for the Easter party!

He's a lot of fun!

What is big and purple and comes
to your house at Easter?

The Easter Barney!

What does the Easter Bunny
think of Easter?

He thinks it's eggs-cellent!

Knock knock.

Who's there?

Carmen.

Carmen who?

Carmen get your candy!

Candy for sale! Great prices!

Knock knock.

Who's there?

Abby.

Abby who?

Abby Easter! Let's celebrate!

Knock knock.

Who's there?

Summer.

Summer who?

Summer my friends don't like chocolate. I love it! How about you?

Why can the Easter Bunny hear
things from a mile away?

He's all ears!

Why did the bunny build
herself a new house?

She was fed up with the hole thing!

Knock knock.

Who's there?

Zookeeper.

Zookeeper who?

Zookeeper way from my candy!

I need it for my lunch tomorrow!

Call the police!

Knock knock.

Who's there?

Owl.

Owl who?

Owl always love Easter Eggs!

They are sooo yummy!

Knock knock.

Who's there?

Norma Lee.

Norma Lee who?

Norma Lee I get full from 1 egg

but today I've had 3!

When did the Easter egg wake up?
The crack of dawn!

What did the Easter Bunny say
after he burped?
Eggs-cuse me!

Knock knock.

Who's there?

Pasta.

Pasta who?

It's Pasta your bedtime!

Lucky we stay up late at Easter!

Knock knock.

Who's there?

Irish.

Irish who?

Irish I knew where the biggest Easter egg is hidden! Yummmmy!

Knock knock.

Who's there?

Myth.

Myth who?

I myth Easter tho much! How about you?

What do you call two rabbits
racing down the road?

The fast and the furriest!

What did the Easter Bunny eat
on a really hot day?

A hop-sicle!

Knock knock.

Who's there?

Amos.

Amos who?

Amos say that candy looks tasty!

Can I eat it all right now?

Knock knock.

Who's there?

Stella.

Stella who?

Let's Stella 'nother Easter joke!

Ha! Ha! Ha!

Knock knock.

Who's there?

Rabbit.

Rabbit who?

Rabbit up neatly please.

It's an Easter present!

What do you call a balloon
made of candy?

A lolli-pop!

Why are rabbits so lucky?

They have four rabbit's feet!

Knock knock.

Who's there?

Waiter.

Waiter who?

Waiter I tell your mom!

You ate 15 eggs!

Knock knock.

Who's there?

Sonia.

Sonia who?

Sonia shoe! Melted chocolate!

Ewwww!

Knock knock.

Who's there?

Bean.

Bean who?

Bean waiting here for ages!

Why are you always late for Easter?

Why did the Easter Egg go down the hill?
To be an egg roll!

Why did the Easter Bunny become a pilot?
To join the hare force!

Knock knock.

Who's there?

Thumb.

Thumb who?

Thumb Easter eggs fell off the porch!

Noooooo!

Knock knock.

Who's there?

Bat.

Bat who?

**Bat you will never guess who
gave me this candy?**

Aunt Betty!

Knock knock.

Who's there?

Beth.

Beth who?

**Beth friends stick together so
let's share our candy!**

What music does the Easter Bunny listen to?

Hip hop!

What do you call a bunny transformer?

Hop-timus Prime!

Knock knock.

Who's there?

Witches.

Witches who?

Witches the best way to

hunt for the eggs?

Knock knock.

Who's there?

Anita.

Anita who?

Anita new Easter basket!

The handle broke! Nooooo!

Knock knock.

Who's there?

Tommy.

Tommy who?

My Tommy is too full!

I ate too much candy!

Crazy Easter Jokes!

Which candy makes you scratch?
Licor-itch!

What do you call a cold dog
sitting on a rabbit?
A chili dog on a bun!

Knock knock.

Who's there?

Army.

Army who?

Army and you still going to

share our candy? Yummy!

Knock knock.

Who's there?

Wire.

Wire who?

Wire all the best eggs so hard to find? Whyyyy??!!

Knock knock.

Who's there?

Venice.

Venice who?

Venice the Easter egg hunt starting? I'm really hungry!

Knock knock.

Who's there?

Cher.

Cher who?

Cher would like to meet the Easter Bunny. Do you know where he lives?

Knock knock.

Who's there?

Dwayne.

Dwayne who?

Dwayne the pool quickly!

My Easter eggs fell in!

Noooooo!

Where do Easter bunnies go to dance?
The Basket ball!

Why is a rabbit like a penny?
Because it has a head on one end
and a tail on the other!

Knock knock.
Who's there?
Jimmy.
Jimmy who?
Jimmy 2 seconds and I will show
you where the eggs are!

Knock knock.

Who's there?

Sarah.

Sarah who?

Is Sarah another way we can

find the Easter eggs?

Knock knock.

Who's there?

Carrie.

Carrie who?

Can you Carrie my

Easter Basket please?

It's way too heavy for me!

What's the Easter Bunny's favorite candy?
Lollihops!

How did the Easter Bunny feel
when he hurt his leg?
Un-hoppy!

Knock knock.

Who's there?

Petunia.

Petunia who?

Petunia shoes!

Let's join the Easter Egg hunt!

Knock knock.

Who's there?

Emerson.

Emerson who?

Emerson nice Easter eggs you have there. Did you get them at Kmart?

Knock knock.

Who's there?

Izzy.

Izzy who?

Izzy Easter egg hunt still on?

I took 4 buses to get here!

When does the Easter Bunny go exactly as fast as a train?
When he's on the train!

What do you call a dumb bunny?
A hare brain!

Knock knock.

Who's there?

Jester.

Jester who?

Jester minute!

Where's all my candy?

Call the police!

Knock knock.

Who's there?

Doughnut.

Doughnut who?

I Doughnut know if I can eat any more candy! I'm going to explode!

Knock knock.

Who's there?

Iran.

Iran who?

Iran really fast to get here and all the candy's gone! Nooooo!

Where do rabbits go if they lose their tails?
A re-tail shop!

Why did the Easter Bunny cross the road?
The chicken was sick!

Knock knock.

Who's there?

Wanda.

Wanda who?

I Wanda if I can buy more Easter eggs with all this money my aunt gave me?

Knock knock.

Who's there?

Des.

Des who?

Des no way I can carry this basket!

Help!

Knock knock.

Who's there?

Olive.

Olive who?

Olive here but I forgot where

I hid the candy!

Where does the Easter Bunny get his eggs?
Eggplants!

What did the Easter Bunny
say on January the 1st?
Hoppy New Year!

Knock knock.

Who's there?

Gwen.

Gwen who?

Gwen you have finished your candy,

let's eat some more!

Knock knock.

Who's there?

Heidi.

Heidi who?

Heidi Easter eggs under the couch!

No-one will find them there!

Knock knock.

Who's there?

Jess.

Jess who?

Jess let me in please!

I need chocolate!

How is a rabbit like a cornstalk?
They both have big ears!

What did prehistoric rabbits use
to cut down trees?
A dino-saw!

Knock knock.

Who's there?

Snow.

Snow who?

Snow use asking me!

I'm 100 years old and can't even

remember what Easter is!

Knock knock.

Who's there?

Justin.

Justin who?

Justin time for chocolate!

I'm soooooo hungry!

Knock knock.

Who's there?

Donna.

Donna who?

Donna want to make a big deal about

it but the Easter Bunny is here!

Why do Easter Bunny's kids
like watching cartoons?
They always end hoppily!

What did the Easter Bunny say to the frog?
Rabbit, rabbit, rabbit!

Knock knock.

Who's there?

Attilla.

Attilla who?

Attilla you what!

I'll swap you this 1 candy for

5 of yours! Good deal!

Knock knock.

Who's there?

Icing.

Icing who?

Icing many Easter songs.

Would you like to hear one?

Knock knock.

Who's there?

Utah.

Utah who?

Utah one who asked me over!

Let's find all the candy!

How do you know carrots are good for your eyes?

Did you ever see a bunny with glasses?

What's the name of the bunny who stole from the rich and gave to the poor?

Rabbit Hood!

Knock knock.

Who's there?

Renata.

Renata who?

Renata candy!

Nooooo!

Knock knock.

Who's there?

Harley.

Harley who?

Harley ever see you nowadays!

Are you back for Easter?

How are the kids?

Knock knock.

Who's there?

Frankfurter.

Frankfurter who?

Frankfurter Easter Egg!

You are too kind!

Hilarious Easter Jokes!

How do you know where Easter Bunny is?
Eggs marks the spot!

What did the carrot say to the Bunny?
Do you want to grab a bite?

Knock knock.

Who's there?

Dishes.

Dishes who?

Dishes the police! Open up!

Are you the Easter Bunny?

Knock knock.

Who's there?

Taco.

Taco who?

I want to Taco bout why

I love chocolate.

Do you have a spare 3 hours?

Knock knock.

Who's there?

Some Bunny.

Some Bunny who?

Some Bunny has eaten

my Easter Eggs!

Nooooo!

What game does Easter Bunny play?

Hop scotch!

What do you get when you pour hot water down a rabbit hole?

A hot cross bunny!

Knock knock.

Who's there?

Avenue.

Avenue who?

Avenue seen the news!

Easter Bunny is here!

Knock knock.

Who's there?

Randy.

Randy who?

Randy whole way from my house!

Let's eat candy!

Knock knock.

Who's there?

Ogre.

Ogre who?

Can you come Ogre for

dinner tonight?

We're having candy on toast!

What do you get when you cross
a frog with a rabbit?

A bunny ribbit!

What did the rabbit say to
the Easter Bunny?

Hi dad!

Knock knock.

Who's there?

Lava.

Lava who?

I Lava Easter so much!

Candy! Yummm!

Knock knock.

Who's there?

Obi wan.

Obi wan who?

Obi Wan of your best friends!

Let's eat all of your chocolates!

Knock knock.

Who's there?

Ears.

Ears who?

Ears hoping you have an

eggs-cellent Easter!!

Why did the Easter Bunny spread the eggs all over the yard?
He didn't want all his

eggs in one basket!

What job do rabbits at hotels have?
Bellhop!

Knock knock.

Who's there?

Eddy.

Eddy who?

Eddy body home?

I have spare candy!

Knock knock.

Who's there?

Guess Simon.

Guess Simon who?

Guess Simon the wrong place!

Are you the Easter Bunny?

Knock knock.

Who's there?

Honey bee.

Honey bee who?

Honey bee kind and get your grandma some chocolate!

Why was the Easter egg hiding
under the sofa?
It was a little chicken!

Why is the Easter Bunny so fit?
He gets lots of eggs-ercise!

Knock knock.

Who's there?

Candy.

Candy who?

Candy person who stole my chocolate

give it back please?

Knock knock.

Who's there?

Ivan.

Ivan who?

Ivan interview with the Easter Bunny for channel 7 news!

Yayyy!

Knock knock.

Who's there?

Norway.

Norway who?

That's Norway to eat an Easter egg!

Here, let me show you how!

Why did the bunny get so mad?
She was having a bad hare day!

How did the Easter Bunny get so rich?
He ate lots of Fortune Cookies!

Knock knock.

Who's there?

Candice.

Candice who?

Candice Easter basket

get any heavier?

I can hardly lift it!

Knock knock.

Who's there?

Dewey.

Dewey who?

Dewey have to eat all the

eggs at once? I'm full!

Knock knock.

Who's there?

Henrietta.

Henrietta who?

Henrietta too mucha candy!

He looks a bit green!

Why did the Easter Bunny go to hospital?
To get a hopperation!

Where did the Easter Bunny go after he was married?
On his bunnymoon!

Knock knock.

Who's there?

Whale.

Whale who?

Whale I'll be!

Grandma ate all the Easter eggs!

Knock knock.

Who's there?

Sweet Tea.

Sweet Tea who?

Please be a Sweet Tea and give grandma a candy!

Knock knock.

Who's there?

Icy.

Icy who?

Icy you have the biggest Easter egg! Can I have it?

Why did the Easter Bunny jump
out of a plane?
To try eggs-treme sports!

What do you call a really smart rabbit?
A hare brain!

Knock knock.

Who's there?

Frank.

Frank who?

Frank you very much for all this

candy! No wonder I love you!.

Knock knock.

Who's there?

Gopher.

Gopher who?

Gopher help quick!

The Easter Bunny fell

down the stairs!

Knock knock.

Who's there?

Wendy.

Wendy who?

Wendy Easter Bunny gets here please

wake me up! Goodnight!

What do rabbits have that nothing else in the entire world has?

Baby rabbits!

What did the taxi driver say to the Easter Bunny?

Hop in!

Knock knock.

Who's there?

Gladys.

Gladys who?

Gladys Easter! I love candy!

Can I eat all of yours?

Knock knock.

Who's there?

King Tut.

King Tut who?

King Tut key fried chicken for

Easter dinner tonight!

Yummy!

Knock knock.

Who's there?

Cheese.

Cheese who?

Cheese very good at finding eggs.

Her dad taught her!

Funnier Easter Jokes!

What do you call the bunny that comes 3 days after Easter?

Choco Late!

What do skunks get for Easter?

Smelly beans!

Knock knock.

Who's there?

Oliver.

Oliver who?

Oliver other kids are busy so

can you help me eat this

huge bag of candy?

Knock knock.

Who's there?

Robin.

Robin who?

Robin you!

Hands up and give me your candy!

Knock knock.

Who's there?

Sawyer.

Sawyer who?

Sawyer were having an

Easter egg hunt!

Can we join in?

What do bunnies sing at birthday parties?
Hoppy birthday to you!

How can you catch the Easter Bunny?
Hide in the garden and make a noise like a carrot!

Knock knock.
Who's there?
Alma.
Alma who?
Alma Easter candy has gone!
Nooooo!

Knock knock.

Who's there?

Voodoo.

Voodoo who?

Voodoo you think it is knocking?

The Easter Bunny?

Knock knock.

Who's there?

Terrain.

Terrain who?

It's starting terrain!

The candy's getting wet!

Nooooooo!

Knock knock.

Who's there?

West.

West who?

If you need a West from eating your candy I can eat it for you!

Knock knock.

Who's there?

Soda.

Soda who?

Soda you want another Easter Egg? I have 3 spare ones!

Why did the Easter Bunny cross the road?
No bunny knows!

What did Santa Claus get for Easter?
Jolly Beans!

Knock knock.

Who's there?

Phil.

Phil who?

Phil my Easter basket please!

I'm so hungry!

Knock knock.

Who's there?

Nanna.

Nanna who?

Nanna your business!

The Easter egg hunt is top secret!

Knock knock.

Who's there?

Sofa.

Sofa who?

Sofa I've got 12 Easter eggs!

Should last me 3 weeks!

If a freezing cold dog sits on a bunny, what is it?

A chili dog on a bun!

Why did the Easter Bunny fall asleep?

He was eggs-hausted!

Knock knock.

Who's there?

Peas.

Peas who?

Peas help me carry my basket!

It's sooo heavy!

Knock knock.

Who's there?

Omelette.

Omelette who?

Omelette ing you come to my Easter party if you open the door!

Knock knock.

Who's there?

Kent.

Kent who?

Kent you see I like candy!

Can I eat yours?

Pretty Please?

What do you call a rabbit with fleas?
Bugs Bunny!

Why was the Easter egg sad
after telling a joke?
She cracked up!

Knock knock.

Who's there?

Howard.

Howard who?

Howard you like to help me eat

all these Easter Eggs?

I'm full!

Knock knock.

Who's there?

Ferdie.

Ferdie who?

Ferdie last time please open up!

It's the Easter Bunny!

Knock knock.

Who's there?

Al.

Al who?

Al be so happy when you open the door and we eat all these Easter eggs!

Do you think 27 is enough?

Thank You

......So much for reading our book!

We hope you have had a whole bunch of laughs and giggles and enjoyed reading our book.

If you could let us know what you thought of our book by leaving a review we would appreciate it so much!

We have made it really easy to leave a review.

Just go to jackyjay.com anytime!

If you like, you can also check out all the latest books while you are there.

Thanks again and we hope you have a very Happy Easter!
Yours truly,

Jacky Jay